CW00840119

Alison is a new children's author based in Wiltshire.

With a career background in the corporate world, Alison felt that she had something to share with young people everywhere.

"With increasing pressure all around our children today, it is important that we allow them the space to use their imagination and be creative. At the same time, we need to share important messages."

Loz – The Worry-Eating Monster is the first of a set of books with underlying themes to support the mental health of our children, from sharing worries or anxieties, reporting bullying and dealing with disabilities.

LOZ
The Worry-Eating Monster

Loz loved to eat worries.
Loz was a worry-eating monster.

Alison McQuillan

AUSTIN MACAULEY PUBLISHERS™

LONDON ★ CAMBRIDGE ★ NEW YORK ★ SHARJAH

A CIP catalogue record for this title is available from the British Library.

ISBN 9781528916943 (Paperback)
ISBN 9781528916950 (Kindle e-book)
ISBN 9781528961738 (ePub e-book)
www.austinmacauley.com

First Published (2019)
Austin Macauley Publishers Ltd
25 Canada Square
Canary Wharf
London
E14 5LQ

Dedicated to my goddaughter, Harriet; and my niece, Evie – the future generation.

To my mum, for always believing in me; you were my inspiration.

Loz was big and round, with fur the colours of the rainbow – red, yellow, pink, green, orange, purple and blue. He had blue pointed ears like an elf and big blue feet with curly blue toes. But the special thing about Loz was the zip he had for a mouth.

You see, Loz had a very special job. His job was to eat children's worries.

Loz loved to eat worries – little worries, big worries, worries about food, worries about school, worries about almost everything.

Every night, Loz would sit on his special seat in the forest and
wait for the special sound, the sound that told him that there
were worries to eat – the tinkling of silver bells.
Loz loved his special chair; it was made out of the trunk of
the oldest oak tree in the forest; big branches made the chair's
arms, and his big feet rested on a small green bush. His chair
was perfectly placed, deep in the centre of the forest, to hear
the tinkling of the silver bells.
This day, Loz was sitting in his chair, brushing his coloured
fur and humming to himself when he heard the sound –

yes! It was the tinkling of silver bells.

"Great!" shouted Loz, jumping out of his chair, "That means that I have worries to eat, I love collecting and eating worries."

He jumped down from his chair and began running towards the sound of the bells.

"No time to lose," said Loz.

With a quick rub of his pointy ears, Loz disappeared in a puff of coloured smoke.

Pooof!

Poofff!

He had arrived. He was looking at a small white house with a green front door. "Hmmm," said Loz thoughtfully, rubbing his chin. "I wonder who lives here."

With another rub of his ears, poooof!!! He was in Sarah's bedroom.

Now, Loz was such a special worry-eating monster — he could visit any house and visit any child but stay completely invisible till he was ready to show himself. "Heehee, don't want to surprise anyone," chuckled Loz.

Sarah was crying.

"Oh my," sobbed Loz, "seeing a child cry makes me cry." Sniff, sniff.

Poooof!!!

Loz was suddenly visible, standing in front of Sarah. She looked up and immediately stopped crying, her eyes wide with surprise.

"Who are you?" Sarah sniffed, "Why are you in my bedroom!"

Loz was embarrassed. He shuffled his big blue feet and twisted the coloured fur on his tummy.

"I'm Loz!" he shouted proudly. "I eat worries, you look like you have worries that need to be eaten and taken away, I can help you."

"No one can help me," sobbed Sarah. "Everything is ruined, I will never stop crying – ever!"

"Ohh!" said Loz. He rubbed his chin again thoughtfully.

Sarah was very upset.

Suddenly, Loz stopped dancing.

"What are you worried about?" said Loz.

Sarah sat on the edge of the bed, with her head in her hands.

"I'm sad because my mummy and daddy are not going to live together anymore," Sarah sighed. Sarah was so worried.

She didn't want to leave the house she had always known, or think about Daddy living somewhere else. What if he forgot about her?

"Don't worry," said Loz, "let's write your worries down, and I can eat them and tuck them away in my tummy, and you don't have to worry anymore. I will eat your worries away, I promise," said Loz.

Sarah picked up her pencil and began to write. She wrote for a long time. Loz sat patiently and waited – and waited.

"All done!" she exclaimed.

"OK, tuck them in my mouth," said Loz. He zipped up his mouth and swallowed.

"All gone, all safely eaten and tucked away," said Loz, rubbing his big, round tummy.

"Thank you, thank you," said Sarah excitedly, "I feel better already." She gave Loz a great big hug.

"That tickles," he chuckled.

Suddenly, Loz heard tinkling silver bells. "It's time for me to go," said Loz, "I have other worries to eat; other children need my help."

"Oh," said Sarah, "I'm sorry that you have to go."

Sarah was very sad.

Sarah looked at Loz thoughtfully. "How do you know when there are children with worries to eat?" asked Sarah.

She stared at Loz.

"No one has ever asked me that before," said Loz.

23

Mmmm!
Yummy!

Loz sat down crossed-legged on Sarah's bedroom floor. "I know when there are worries to eat because I hear the sound of tinkling silver bells," said Loz. "I have a special seat in the forest where I sit and listen, and when I hear the bells, I come running!" said Loz excitedly.

"You must be very busy," said Sarah.

"Yes, I am, but I love eating the worries away for children; I am the best worry-eating monster in the whole world!" said Loz, jumping up and spinning round and round.

Sarah giggled as she watched Loz spinning. "Where do the worries you eat go?"

Loz stopped spinning. "Well, when I have finished eating all the worries, I go back to my special seat in the forest, then I

rub my tummy, there's a big burp and the worries fly from my mouth as coloured bubbles – hundreds of them!"

"Bubbles don't come out of my mouth when I burp!" said Sarah, staring at Loz.

"Heehee, no, that's a special trick just for me! All the bubbles float up to the sky and disappear."

The sound of tinkling silver bells grew louder.

"Have to go!" said Loz. He gave Sarah a big hug and with a rub of his blue ears, Poooof!!! He was gone.

Left behind where Loz had been sitting was a card. Sarah picked up the card and started to read.

"Remember when you look up to the sky
A coloured rainbow you may spy.
People think that rain makes rainbows bright and clear
But the secret is that all those coloured bubbles that I burp
They make a big, bright rainbow suddenly appear!
Love, Loz."

Sarah hugged the card close to her chest and tucked it safely under her pillow.

So, every time you see a rainbow in the sky, remember that is just all the worries that Loz has eaten for all the children of the world. What a very clever worry-eating monster. The best in the world!

THE END